The Gift

By C.W. Pearson

The Gift

Written By
C.W. Pearson

Foreword By
Robby Robinson

ISBN: 979-8-9999853-1-6

Printed in the United States of America

CEDA'S
PUBLISHING HOUSE

Foreword

By Robby Robinson

I've known Pastor Chuck Pearson for well over a decade now, long enough to say this with confidence: he is one of those rare people whose faith shows up, not just in what he says, but in how he lives.

Chuck is a great man of God, but he is also a musician, artist, craftsman, and storyteller. More importantly, he is someone who truly loves his Lord, truly loves people, and truly loves sharing God's love in everything he does. That combination isn't common and when you encounter it, you feel it almost immediately.

That's one of the reasons Chuck has been such a blessing to *Jam' n Java* from its earliest days. Long before it became a podcast, during our Monday night jam sessions, Chuck was there…offering wisdom, prayer, and encouragement with humility and grace.

He has a gift for speaking truth, without pressure, for sharing Scripture without pretense, and for meeting people exactly where they are. He's also one of those guys you just love hanging around with. Conversations with Chuck can move effortlessly from faith to music to art to life…often in the same breath. And yes, I love him as a brother. The only thing we don't see eye to-eye on is baseball teams…but I've chosen to forgive him for that.

The Gift is a Christmas story - but it's also much more than that. It reminds us that God's greatest gifts are often wrapped in ways we don't expect, delivered in moments we would never choose, and revealed through people who simply show up with love. My prayer is that as you read this story, you won't just understand the gift…you'll receive it.

Dedication

The Apostle James wrote, *"Every good and perfect gift is from above, coming down from the Father of the heavenly lights, who does not change like shifting shadows." (James 1:7).*

And the Apostle Peter wrote, *"Each of you should use whatever gift you have received to serve others, as faithful stewards of God's grace in its various forms." (1 Peter 4:10).*

My life has been filled with an abundance of God's gifts. Some of them are easily recognizable; my faith, my wife, Marseda, my children, my grandchildren, my family, my faithful friends, such as Robby Robinson, and the churches I have been blessed to serve. Sometimes, however, His gifts aren't that easy to recognize or don't seem "good" or "perfect."

This story is dedicated to **Him** who is the author of, *"every good and perfect gift"*, even the ones we don't recognize, and to my wife, Marseda, our six children (Chuck, Jani, Andrew, Becky, Mike and Kristi), the four greatest grandchildren in the world (Abby, Amelia, Will and Audrey), my friends, and my church family spread across America.

I have been blessed to serve as your Pastor and your Brother-in-Christ.

Soli Deo Gloria
C.W. Pearson

It was cold...

Paul Franklin *sat* in the right rear passenger seat of his car looking out of windows that were frosted over, despite the heater running at full blast. James, his chauffeur, sat in the driver's seat, waiting.

It was time. In fact, it was past time. He knew, in the depths of his heart, that he could not put it off any longer. Still, he didn't move. It seemed so final. He was afraid. There was no getting past it. He was more afraid and uncertain about this than he had been of anything in the last twenty years. His life was not without victories. He had overcome many hardships, many difficulties, and many struggles. And yet...

It was time.

The chances he would overcome this battle, this enemy, were not good. But they had said there was a chance.

He shifted in his seat. He looked at his chauffeur. "It's time James" he said. "Past time."

"Very good sir." James said. James opened his own door, moved to the door beside him and opened it.

"Let me get your luggage, Sir", he said.

"No," he answered. "Thank you, but this is a journey I have to make by myself."

James looked hesitant. "Certainly, I can carry your luggage inside, Sir", he said. There was pain in his voice.

8

They had been together for more than 30 years. More than a chauffeur, James had become a friend, and his confidant. There were times when they had stayed up talking over a beer or a cup of coffee late into the night. Sometimes it was about life. At other times it was about upcoming business deals or a trip he had to go on. But always he could count on James to be there with him, beside him.

"Are you sure?" James asked. Pausing, he added, "Paul?"

James seldom called him by his first name. When they were alone and talking about life or their hopes for the future, they were on a first name basis. But James believed in a strict professional relationship even though they were more than employer and employee.

He looked at James. "Thank you, my friend", he said and reached out touching him on the shoulder. "But..." His voice trailed away.

"I understand, Sir", James said. James handed him his suitcase and turned to walk to the car. As he reached the driver's side door of the car, James stopped and looked back to him. There was a tear running down his cheek.

"If there's anything, Sir", he said softly.

Paul nodded but did not say anything. He couldn't. There was too much emotion inside his chest, so he turned and walked into the building. He let the heavy glass door close behind him and turned and faced the front desk. As he approached the woman behind the front desk smiled and asked for his name. He gave it and she smiled and handed him some forms to be filled out. "I know you have already filled out a lot of papers, Sir. But there are a few more bits of information we need", she said apologetically.

He smiled as best as he could and took them without complaint. He sat at the desk and filled them out. When he was finished, she thanked him and turned to one of the nurses standing there. "Room 23", she said.

The nurse smiled at him and said, "Would you follow me sir?" She led him to the elevator and then to his room.

It was a simple room with his bed, and a chair facing a large window. The curtains were drawn against the cold. There was a telephone, and a television. The nurse went through the directions for the television and showed him how to call the nurses' desk if he needed anything.

"Doctor Gottes will be in to see you in about half an hour Mr. Franklin. He asked that you change out of your regular clothes and into the hospital gown in the closet. There is a robe there for you also."

"Is there anything I can get you before I leave?", she asked.

"No," he said with a sigh "I'm fine for now."

He changed into the gown, put on the robe, and hung his clothes in the closet. He looked at his watch. It was a force of habit for him. He had always needed to adhere to a strict schedule. Not much longer, he thought. Well, maybe in the future. But...

His thoughts trailed off.

He walked to the window and drew open the curtain. The edges of the window were covered with frost, and he could hardly see out of it. As if through an old window filled with imperfect glass, he saw a park across the street from where the hospital was located. And across from that, was a church. He wondered what time the services were scheduled for. It was a bitter night for anyone who would dare to venture out.

A few moments later the Doctor came into his room. He told him about all the tests they were going to run and how long each one should take. Mentally, he figured he would be occupied the rest of the day.

Later, when he got back to his room, dinner was waiting for him. But he wasn't very hungry. He drank some coffee and ate a slice of bread with some kind of butter substitute. That was about all he wanted.

He turned on the television, wondering if the local football team had managed to win that afternoon. But sports weren't on yet. So, he turned it off and pulled out a book he had brought with him. But he couldn't concentrate, so he sat looking out the window of his room, lost in the numbness and shock. And then he was aware that he wasn't alone. A woman had come into his room and stood beside him looking out of the window.

"Hi!", she said in a voice that was as cheery as she could make it. "My name is Patty. What's yours?"

Her greeting had broken his reverie.

"What?", he snapped at her.

"I said my name is Patty and asked what yours is." She said a little louder than she had before.

"Paul", he said, but with a tone of voice that left no doubt in her mind that he was not in a receptive mood. He was sullen and grumpy.

He noticed she was dressed exactly as he was. She was a fellow patient then. He snapped at her, "I left orders that I didn't want to be disturbed. What are you doing in my room?"

Her smile never wavered. "I know you did, Paul. I came to welcome you to the ward. I like to welcome all the new patients."

"Good for you!", Paul thought to himself. "How about you leave me alone!"

"I thought maybe it would be a good time to talk and get to know each other." Patty continued. "It could help pass the time."

He looked at her more closely. She was wearing a faded red robe over her pajamas. She had blond hair, and as he looked at her face, he noticed her deep blue eyes. She was an older woman, and once she might have been thought of as pretty. But now her face was drawn, and she was very thin and frail looking. The thing that struck him however was her smile, which seemed to light up her whole body.

"Why?", Paul asked as he turned his attention back to the window. He really wanted nothing to do with her or anyone else for that matter. He just wanted to be left alone.

"Why what?", Patty asked.

"Why do you visit all the patients?", Paul asked.

She didn't answer right away.

She studied him for a moment. Then she sighed and said, "Well, sometimes people who come here have a lot of questions, or they are afraid and uncertain. I just like to meet them and let them know I care, and I'm available if they want to talk."

Paul said nothing. He certainly wasn't going to open up to some strange woman about everything he was going through. It had been difficult enough to tell James what he was facing. Let her in on his fears and uncertainty? There was no way he would do that! Besides, he suspected there was more to it than her "caring" about him. People didn't "care" for strangers or people they hardly knew. Sometimes your own family didn't really "care" about you. He had found that out the hard way.

Patty smiled at him. "I can tell you have a lot on your mind", she said. She turned toward the door and said cheerfully, "I'll see you later." Then she added, "I'm in room #14 just down the hall if you need anything."

"Okay. Thank you", Paul said dully, "but I'm fine."

"Okay", Patty said. "I'll see you tomorrow."

Paul was hoping she would forget about him and leave him alone. A lot of people made promises to him that they never kept. His wife, his son...

But that wasn't fair. They were gone, yes, and it still hurt. His wife and their son had been on the way home so they might begin the process of reconciliation. That's when the news came about the plane crash. He never had a chance to tell her how sorry he was. He had said it, over the phone. But he had wanted to show her - to show Tommy that he loved him. But the plane had gone down...

He had dealt with their deaths by losing himself in his business. It was ironic that the very thing that had brought on their separation was the very thing in which he could now take comfort. He had tried not to shut out his close friends or the friends he and Betty had. But in time, they all drifted apart. Except for James. And one or two other men at the club. But one of them had died of a heart attack a couple of years ago, and the other was in a facility for people suffering from dementia. Paul had gone to visit him a time or two. But the last time, Ralph didn't recognize him. Ruth, his wife, had told him that Ralph didn't recognize her, or their children either.

Outside, in the park across the street, children were playing in the snow. Some were making a snowman. Others were having a snowball fight, and younger children were enjoying being pulled through the park on a sled by their older siblings or parents.

14

On the other side of the park, clearly in view, was a church. It was decorated for the Christmas season. One of the nurses had told him that he would be able to hear the chimes from the church's carillon twice a day; at eight in the morning and five in the afternoon.

The wind howled around the eves of the building. The lights in the corridor outside his room were turned down and a nurse came into his room. She was young. She smiled and said, "Mr. Franklin, it's time for bed. The doctor told me you could have a sedative if you felt you needed it."

"No," Paul said, "It's been a long day, and I think I'll sleep okay."

She helped him get under the covers, handed him the call button, and closed the door as she turned out the lights.

"Just call me if you change your mind", she said softly.

"Okay." Paul answered. But he knew he wouldn't call.

He lay there for a while, but sleep wouldn't come. His mind was too active. He thought of his wife and son. He thought of all he had gained in life, and how at this point, it didn't hold much value for him. Maybe there was hope. Dr. Gottes had implied there was always new research and new developments, but...

Sometime later he awoke. The room was cold. He had to go to the bathroom. He sighed. He didn't want to get up, but his bladder wouldn't let him stay in bed.

"The curse of being old" he told himself. It was a joke he and James had told each other time and again as they both suffered from late night or early morning calls from "mother nature."

When he got back into bed, he called the nurse and asked for another blanket. She returned with one quickly.

"I warmed it for you Mr. Franklin" she said with a smile.

The next thing he knew he was fast asleep. The next morning the orderly woke him with his breakfast.

"Good morning, Mr. Franklin", he said cheerily. "New day is upon us. I brought your breakfast." He put it on the tray next to Paul's bed. "Would you like me to help you sit up?"

Paul never woke up easily. I'd like to be left alone!" He said grumpily. And then felt guilty. "I'm sorry", he said. "I've just never been one to wake up very happy!" he explained. "Actually, I need to head to the bathroom", he said.

"I understand completely", the orderly said as he helped Paul out of bed and into his robe. When Paul returned, the orderly asked him, "Would you rather eat breakfast sitting on your bed or looking out the window?"

Paul thought about it. "Let's go to the window. Maybe I can see something this morning."

"Good enough!", said the orderly as he set the breakfast tray on the stand and adjusted it so Paul could eat it. Then the orderly opened the curtains.

The sun shone brightly. It seemed the wind had blown the storm out of town. It was a beautiful day.

"Anything else I can get for you Mr. Franklin?", the orderly asked.

"No, I don't think so. Thank you", Paul said. Then added, "Any word on how the Lancers did last night?"

"Yes", the orderly answered enthusiastically. "They pulled it out in the fourth quarter. Engers hit Wilson with pass in the end zone with 13 seconds to go!"

"That's great!", Paul said with a smile.

"Sure is", said the orderly. "I won forty bucks on the game. Friend of mine said Engers was over the hill!"

"Yes", Paul answered. "My lawyer said the same thing. Guess I should have made him put his money where his mouth is!"

They both laughed. The orderly left and Paul turned to his breakfast and looked out the window.

A lot of snow had fallen last night. The park lay covered with a white blanket that sparkled like crystal in the sunlight. It almost hurt Paul's eyes.

He noticed that on the other side of the park the church's outdoor creche lay covered with snow. He was amused with Mary, Joseph and the Baby

Jesus being covered with at least three inches of the stuff.

Breakfast was nothing very memorable. "Hospital food," he said to himself. The coffee was cold, as were the eggs. The toast was soggy and the hash browns - well, better off left on the tray.

In the park, the local children gathered to play. He watched them as they built snow forts and battled with snowballs.

"Hi", someone said behind him. He turned and saw Patty.

"Hi", he said without any enthusiasm.

She said nothing more to him, she just came over to the window and stood there, looking at the scene outside. Occasionally, she would laugh at some of the antics of the children as they played in the snow. After what seemed like a long time, she turned to Paul and asked, "How was your night? Did you sleep okay?"

He didn't answer right away. "Okay I guess."

He really didn't feel like being polite, but it was the way he was raised. So, he made the attempt. "Did you sleep okay?", he asked.

"Very well", she answered. "Thank you for asking."

He didn't respond.

After a few moments of silence, she asked, "What's in store for you today?"

He didn't really know. "More tests I guess", he responded.

"I know how that goes", she sighed. "I've been here a couple of weeks, and it seems like they always have a new test, or want more blood, so somehow I need to be poked or prodded in some way every day."

He laughed in spite of himself. "Isn't that the truth!", he said.

"Do you know why you're here?", she asked. "What they're looking for?"

"Yes", he said but fell silent.

She seemed comfortable with the silence. She turned and looked out the window.

"It's tough", she said quietly. "As I said, I've been here for a couple of weeks. All the tests…" her voice trailed off. "The not knowing…", she said even more quietly.

Paul said nothing.

He didn't know how she could zero in on what he was feeling so easily and precisely. The tests he could handle. At least for a while. But the not knowing, the uncertainty, that was the worst of it.

One of the nurses came in and took his tray. "I see you've met Patty", she said to Paul. "Isn't she just a jewel?", she asked smiling.

Patty turned red. Paul said nothing.

As she left, the nurse said, "Dr. Gottes will be in to see you soon."

Patty looked at her as she left the room. "I'll catch you later. Okay?", she said to Paul.

"Sure", Paul said.

As Patty walked to the door he said, "Patty?"

"Yes", she answered.

"I'm sorry.", he said.

"For what?"

"I'm not used to being around people as…" he paused looking for the right word. "Friendly", he said cautiously. "I…It's been a long time…" His voice trailed off.

"I understand Paul. It's okay. I'll see ya later."

"Okay", he said and returned to looking out the window.

The children must have had enough of the cold because the park was now empty. Or maybe, he thought, their mothers had called them home. Hot chocolate sounded good to him. Just looking out the window made him cold.

A few minutes later another nurse came in with a wheelchair.

"More tests?", he asked.

She nodded yes. Then she said, "And I think they have some medication for you too."

"The first step", he said to himself, as he got into the wheelchair.

When he returned to his room, his lunch was waiting for him on the carrier. It sat next to the chair looking out the window. He got out of the wheelchair and walked to the chair. He pulled the tray to him and uncovered it. Lunch was less exciting than breakfast had been. On top of that, it was cold.

He drank the juice, ate the cookie that was supposed to be desert, and started sipping the cold coffee, as he looked out the window.

The children were out in the park again. School must be out he thought to himself. Then, "Well, of course, it's Christmas week", he said to himself. That drew his attention to the church on the other side of the park. Mary, Joseph and the Baby Jesus no longer had their blanket of snow covering them.

Wise Men and shepherds had been added to the creche. As he watched, a couple of men were adding large candles to the Nativity scene. One of them bent over and seemed to work on something behind the creche.

Then, lights began to shine, and he heard the faint sound of music. It was a Christmas carol. He didn't recognize it at first and then realized it had begun playing in the middle of the carol. He recognized the melody of, ***O Little Town Of Bethlehem.***

"It's beautiful, isn't it?", Patty said behind him.

He turned to her. "I suppose", he said. He hadn't had much use for Christmas, or carols, or presents since his wife and son died in that plane crash. He always remembered James with a bonus, of course. And there was the doorman at the hotel where he lived in his penthouse, and his secretary and a few others. But that was a kind of duty.

There was no joy, no sense of enthusiasm in the giving. It was just a necessity, an obligation.

Patty moved next to the window and looked back at him.

"Penny for your thoughts," she said quietly.

He looked up at her and shrugged.

"Not worth the investment", he said with a little smile.

He continued to look out the window.

It seemed so peaceful in the park. Almost a scene worthy of some Christmas card.

The church with the creche added to the scene. And he heard the music being played. It was faint, but he could still hear it. Patty could too. She hummed the melody.

"That's a beautiful carol," she said. "So filled with hope in spite of the pain associated with it."

"What do you mean?", Paul asked.

"It's from a poem written by Walt Whitman I think", she said. Then added, "No, it was Henry Wadsworth Longfellow."

She turned from the window to look at him. "Do you know the words?", she asked.

"Just the beginning", he said singing the melody to himself. "I heard the bells on Christmas Day…Their old familiar carols play…And wild and sweet the words repeat…Of peace on earth, good will to men.", he said, and then paused. "That's about it", he laughed.

Patty began to recite the words…

22

"I thought how, as the day had come,
The belfries of all Christendom
Had rolled along, th' unbroken song
Of peace on earth, good will to men."

"And in despair I bowed my head;
"There is no peace on earth;" I said,
"For hate is strong and mocks the song
Of peace on earth, good will to men."

She paused and looked at him. "Do you know the story behind it?", she asked.

"No.", he said. After she had recited that last stanza, he had thought it matched his mood.

"Peace on earth?", he said to himself. "That's a laugh!"

Patty said, "When he wrote that, Longfellow's life was filled with a lot of pain. His wife had died in a fire a couple of years earlier. Her dress had caught fire when she was lighting candles, and she died the next day from her injuries. Then his son left to join the union army without his blessing. His son had been appointed as a lieutenant and had been severely wounded in some battle. I don't remember which one. But he wrote the poem, in the midst of his grief, over his wife, his uncertainty whether his son would live, and the terrible cost of the Civil War."

"Let me see if I can remember the poem. It's different than the carol.", she added.

"Let's see.", she said.

"Till ringing, singing on its way,
The world revolved from night to day,
A voice, a chime,
A chant sublime
Of peace on earth, good will to men!"

"Then from each black, accursed mouth
The cannon thundered in the South,
And with the sound
The carols drowned
Of peace on earth, good will to men!"

She paused, thinking.

"It was as if an earthquake rent
The hearthstones of a continent,
And made forlorn
The households born
Of peace on earth, good will to men."

"That's where the stanza about bowing his head in despair comes in", she said. The carol doesn't use the three stanzas I just quoted to you."

"I can understand why!" He almost grumbled the words out.

"It seems to me there's too much left out", she said. "But the last one is really important."

"Then pealed the bells, more loud and deep,
God is not dead, nor doth he sleep!
The Wrong shall fail,
The Right prevail,
With peace on earth, good will toward men."

"I guess he found comfort and strength in the midst of all his pain and grief in the Christmas story", she said wistfully.

He said nothing.

They were silent for a long time. Finally, Patty said she was tired and was going to go lie down for a while.

He smiled at her and said he would see her later.

Outside the afternoon became dusk. The lights at the creche twinkled. The carols continued to play. It was Silent Night playing this time.

The nurse brought his dinner. It looked as unappetizing as lunch and breakfast, but he was hungry. So, he ate. Bland vegetables, rubbery meat, mushy "instant" potatoes and coffee that wasn't.

Desert was a stale fortune cookie.

He assumed it was supposed to be healthy - but he doubted it.

He dosed in his chair for a bit.

About 7:00, Patty was back. "Do you play cards?", she asked.

"Not much anymore. Not since…"

His voice trailed away. Not since she died and Tommy with her. Not since he began to isolate himself from all their friends who didn't understand.

She held a deck in her hands.

"Want to play some Gin Rummy?", she asked.

"God, I hate that game!", he said.

His wife had loved it. And she enjoyed clobbering him when they played. He hadn't played it since…

There was that phrase again.

Not since…

"Why not", he said. "Might as well give you a chance to clobber me just like…just like my wife used to."

Patty sensed his pain.

"We don't have play that game. I know a bunch of kid's card games.", said Patty. "I'm an elementary school teacher. Sometimes card games can help teach other things more efficiently."

"I remember my wife teaching my son the game of concentration in order to try to help him focus.", Paul said. Then added, "Rummy is fine. First, one to a hundred - but you have to spot me seventy-five points."

"No way!", Patty complained. "I think you're trying to snooker me!"

He smiled, took the cards, shuffled them and dealt.

The first game didn't last too long. Patty clobbered him worse than his wife used to.

"Maybe I should give you 85 points", she said with a touch of humor.

"Don't get arrogant!", he said with a smile. "Shut up and deal!"

She laughed and dealt.

He did better this game, but it was still embarrassing.

"I don't think your heart is in this", she said gently. "You're distracted."

"I think you're right, Patty", he responded. "And tired. If you don't mind, I think I'll call it a night."

He looked at the clock. It was only 9:00. But he was tired.

Patty excused herself and Paul went to bed.

The next couple of days were pretty much the same, except one day Patty wasn't feeling well, so they spent the afternoon in her room. They had switched card games to crazy 8's. He still lost but was doing marginally better.

Patty was sitting up in her bed as they played cards. It was her turn to deal. As she shuffled the cards she said, "Paul, can I ask you something?"

He knew what was coming and dreaded the thought of having to answer her questions. But she had been so friendly, and he had enjoyed her company, so he thought about it, and said, "Sure, Patty. What do you want to know?"

"I'm assuming we have the same disease - the same blood disorder. Am I right?"

That wasn't what he expected.

He told her the diagnoses Dr. Gottes had made and she nodded positively.

He really didn't want to talk about this either. But he guessed it was better than talking about his wife and son.

"It's strange, isn't it?", Patty went on. "One day you feel fine, and the next you start losing energy, start developing a lot of other symptoms, and then you find out you're going to die."

Paul said nothing.

"Did it hit you as hard as it hit me?", she asked.

"I don't know", he answered. "But it hit me hard. And all these tests…What's the point? I know there isn't much they can do except try to make you comfortable at the end."

He heard the bitterness in his own voice. He didn't like it. It wasn't who he was. Still…

"I asked myself that too, Paul.", Patty said quietly. "They have some powerful new medicine here. Almost seems like there is nothing wrong with you, if you don't push yourself too much. But then, it still ends quickly"…she added quietly.

There was a long pause in the conversation.

"Do you have anyone, Paul? Anyone who cares about you? Anyone who will miss you?"

"Not really", he said. "My secretary. She's been with me a long time. And James - he's my chauffeur and butler. But he's really the closest friend I have."

"You mentioned your wife - and used the past tense. Aren't you close anymore?", asked Patty.

He looked at her. His chest was tight, and his throat wasn't going to let him answer that. He hated this reaction because it seemed like weakness.

Patty reached out and touched his arm. "It's okay", she said. "You don't have to answer me."

She sighed and looked at the ceiling. Then she looked back at Paul.

"My brother was killed by a drunk driver when he was 17. I had just graduated from college and was at my first teaching job. I grew up in Colorado, but my first teaching position was in Minnesota, at a wonderful school for gifted children. It hurt so bad when I got the news. He was so young and such a good guy, and I couldn't get away. It hurt my parents too", she continued. "Mom never got over it, and when she developed ovarian cancer, she didn't have the will to fight."

She paused.

A tear ran down her cheek.

"My dad kind of gave up after that.", added Patty. "He died about six months later. Doctor said it was a broken heart. Now…it's just me."

Paul tried to clear his throat. It wouldn't cooperate. His voice sounded like it was filled with gravel as he tried to speak.

"My wife and son died in a plane crash almost twenty years ago, Patty. We had been married 10 years, and I had been taking her for granted. Our son was six years old. She left me and took him with her. More to get my attention than anything else, I think. It worked. I realized how much I had made my business the center of my life. But I also realized how much I loved and needed her. My business was important, but she and Tommy were really the ones who kept me centered.", said Paul.

29

He paused.

"Tommy was only 6 years old. And I really didn't know him very well. I had ignored him.", he said quietly.

There was deep silence between them.

Down the hall a patient called out the name "Justin." And repeated it in tears.

Neither Patty nor Paul said anything.

Finally, Paul got up.

"I guess it's time I head to my own room Patty. I'll see you in the morning."

"Okay", she said weakly. "But before you go, you know tomorrow is Christmas Eve, don't you?"

"I guess I hadn't thought about it, Patty. Why do you ask?"

"I wanted to go to Christmas Eve service at the church across the park, but the doctor won't let me. He says I'm too weak. Maybe you want to go."

It was not something he wanted to do. He had sworn off God and religion since…

There was a lot of emotion in his voice as he said, "I don't know Patty. I haven't been to church in years. Not since…" his voice trailed off.

Patty just nodded. She understood.

"Just think about it Paul. Okay?"

He smiled at her.

"Okay." he said as he turned and walked to his room.

He didn't sleep well that night. He dreamed more than he usually did. He saw his wife.

They argued. He said terrible things. She picked up Tommy and jumped out of the window of the penthouse they lived in.

He knew he was dreaming, but it was all too real. He tossed and turned. He was trying to force himself to wake up, but his mind seemed to refuse every attempt.

Monsters of his own creation chased him through ever changing nightmares and he couldn't get away. When he started to wake up, he felt more tired than he had when he went to bed the evening before.

Patty wasn't much better when she came into his room after breakfast. She was in a wheelchair when she came in. She looked haggard and worn. There were dark circles under her eyes.

"Hi, Paul.", she said weakly.

"Hi, yourself", he answered, and then added, "Should you be here? Patty, you don't look so good!"

She smiled.

"Gee, thanks. That's what a girl likes to hear first thing in the morning!"

He blushed. So did she.

"I'm sorry. Paul", she stammered. "I didn't mean anything."

"I know that.", he said softly.

Then he laughed.

"You really zinged me!"

She smiled.

"The doctor said I could come to your room only if the nurse brought me in a wheelchair. So, here I am!", said Patty.

"He also said only for a few moments"...the nurse added.

"Patty...", Paul began.

But she wasn't going to let him say anything.

"Here", she said and handed him a package. "I want you to have this. It's your Christmas present."

It was wrapped in newspaper.

"Patty, I can't...", he said softly.

"Yes, you can and you will," she interrupted. "And none of that you don't have anything for me stuff!"

Her voice was weak but firm.

"But...", he began.

"No buts!", she said firmly. "Paul, I've enjoyed our time together. You're the one friend I have. At least the only one who understands what I'm going through. Please!", she pleaded, "Take this as the gift it is intended to be - the same kind of gift you have been to me."

"But..."

She just pointed a finger at him with a look that said, "No buts! Remember?"

She nodded to the nurse, and they turned to leave Paul's room.

At the door, she turned back and said over her shoulder, "Remember, no peeking! Don't open it until tomorrow on Christmas Day!"

"I'm going to get even!", he said to her defiantly.

"I know!", she responded as the nurse took her down the hall.

And then he was all alone in his room once again.

He looked at the package and placed it on the stand beside the bed.

He looked at the open door to his room, and then at the package, and then back at the door.

He was having trouble trying to figure out what was going on inside of him.

He felt, different, inside.

Why had Patty given him this gift?

She didn't really know him.

They had talked a bit and shared some of the things they had gone through. But there was so much more to knowing a person...wasn't there?

He went back to his chair at the window. In the park the children were having another snowball fight. He laughed at their antics. One little fellow took one right in the face. He could tell it hurt from the boy's reaction. He dropped the snowball in his hand and ran out of the park. Probably on his way home.

Eventually all the children got tired and went home and the park was quiet again.

He just sat there.

Not thinking about anything in particular...but just letting everything he had experienced soak in.

He was still there when lunch came, and he let the tray sit in front of him, while he continued to look out the window. He picked at his food. What he ate was even fairly good. But food wasn't a top priority just now.

He noticed some activity at the church across the park. Several cars pulled into the parking lot. He looked at his watch. It was 2:30 in the afternoon. It was way too early for a Christmas Eve service. Maybe there was a group of people practicing for the service or something.

He turned and went to his bed. He turned on the television looking for something to watch; maybe a movie or a sporting event or something like that. But there was nothing that really interested him.

He lay back in the bed staring at the ceiling.

There was a commotion out in the hall. As he listened, he thought he heard a group of people talking and quietly laughing together. He heard a strange, reedy sound. And then a choir began singing, "Joy to the world, the Lord has come!"

Something happened inside of Paul.

Tears ran down his cheeks. He could tell the choir was walking toward his room. He quickly reached for a Kleenex.

Outside his room, in the hall, the members of the choir began walking past his room. They had finished *"Joy to the World."*

A woman with a beautiful soprano voice began singing, *"What child is This?"*

34

Paul was deeply moved.

One of the choir members, a man, walked into his room and smiled at him.

He reached out and offered to shake hands. Paul took his hand.

"Merry Christmas!", the man said.

"Merry Christmas", Paul answered tearfully.

And then he was gone and the choir moved down the hall.

Soon they had moved to another floor, and the ward grew quiet.

Paul got up and walked down to Patty's room.

She was asleep, so he didn't want to disturb her.

Back in his room he sat down at the window. Below a group of people were walking through the park toward the church.

He recognized one of them - the man who had come into his room and wished him a merry Christmas.

Sometime later the nurse walked in with his medication.

"Tell me about Patty", he said.

"Patty?", the nurse asked. "Well, if anything she seems to be blessed with a real concern for other people and wants to help them adjust to tough situations – like yours. Somehow, it's like she's able to help quite a few people make it through the tough times. She seems to have some kind of gift."

"Gift? What kind of gift?", Paul asked.

"Well," she sighed, "it's kind of hard to explain. It seems Patty has a gift for helping people simply by being with them."

Then she added softly, "Especially in this situation."

Paul said nothing for a moment.

Then he said, "You mean…that just by being with them…what? She's able to help them make it through what they're going through. Through what I'm going through? Dying?"

"Something like that", the nurse answered.

Paul said nothing, but thought to himself, "Is this 'gift' what I have been experiencing all afternoon?"

He didn't think he believed in this kind of stuff. But he couldn't deny the effect Patty had on him.

The nurse recorded Paul's information on the bedside computer.

"Anything I can get for you?", she asked.

Paul shook his head no and muttered a "No, thank you."

"Dinner will be in about an hour or hour and a half.", the nurse said as she walked out of his room.

He had a lot to think about, but he couldn't concentrate, so he got up and walked down the hall to see how Patty was doing.

She was sitting up in bed reading something. She looked up and smiled at him.

"Hi!" she said.

She still looked haggard and worn to him.

"Hi, yourself", he said and pulled the chair next to her bed.

She closed the book she had been reading and put it down on the bed beside her.

"What are you reading?", he asked.

She picked up the book and handed it to him. It was a *Gideon's Bible.*

He handed it back to her without comment.

His facial expression must have betrayed him because she said, "I can tell you're unimpressed Paul. But some days it's the only thing that gives me the strength to keep going."

He said nothing.

Deep down he was afraid she was going to bring up some kind of drivel about heaven and hell. That was the last thing he wanted to hear or talk about.

But she said nothing more, so eventually he was forced to ask the question.

"Patty, what do you mean? Aren't you going to talk to me about some kind of 'eternal destiny' or something?", asked Paul.

Patty laughed.

"No Paul, nothing like that."

"Good!", he said firmly, "because I don't have any interest in any of that religious 'hocus pocus' stuff!"

"Neither do I, Paul.", she said softly. "Neither do I."

They both heard the bells from the church across the park.

It was five o clock.

Paul got up and walked to the window. There weren't any children playing in the park and it looked very cold outside. It looked like the wind was whipping up the snow. He was glad, that for the time being, he was in a place where it was warm.

He looked at the church and saw all the lights and decorations come on.

The thought came to him that maybe he was wrong, and he wondered why he felt so ill at ease when the subject of religion came up.

He turned around to talk to Patty and saw that she was reading the Bible again.

"What are you reading?", he asked her.

"One of my favorite passages, Paul", she said and then asked, "Would you like to read it?"

There was that smile on her face again.

He walked over to Patty and looked at the Bible on her lap.

"I thought you said you didn't have any time for any religious 'hocus pocus,' like me", he said.

There was a threatening accusation in his tone of voice.

"No Paul," she said softly. "That's not quite what I said. I did say that I didn't have time for any religious 'hocus pocus,' not that I don't have time for any religious 'hocus pocus' - like you."

"What's the difference?", he asked sarcastically.

"I have time, Paul, for the real thing", she said gently. "I have a feeling", she continued, "that you don't have time for *anything* in the area of religion or faith."

The sarcasm was still in his voice as he asked, "Aren't you just playing with words? How do you know what the 'real thing' is anyway?"

"I just do, Paul", she said.

Then, getting up she handed him the Bible and said, "Here, read this and tell me what you think."

He looked at the passage she was pointing to. It began, "*We know that in all things God works for good to those who love him, who are called according to his purpose...*"

"You've got to be kidding me!", he said. "You really believe this stuff? With all of the pain and suffering in the world, as well as what you personally have been through? You believe this?"

"I not only believe it, Paul," she said, "I live by it. As I said, it's the only thing that helps me make it through the day, some days."

He looked at her in disbelief. But his eyes were drawn back to the page and he read some more.

"*If God is for us, who can be against us? Certainly not God, who did not even keep back his own Son, but offered Him up for us all! He gave us His Son, will He not also freely give us all things?*

Who can separate us from the love of Christ? Shall tribulation, or distress, or persecution, or famine, or nakedness, or danger, or sword? No, in all these things we are more than conquerors through him who loved us. For I am sure that neither death nor life, nor angels nor rulers, nor things present nor things to come, nor powers, nor height nor depth, nor anything else in all creation, will be able to separate us from the love of God in Christ Jesus our Lord..."

He put the book down.

He had never read anything like this, and he wasn't sure he understood what the passage meant.

"Well, whatever works for you, I guess", he said, trying to pass the whole thing off with an air of nonchalant indifference.

But Patty wasn't buying any of it.

"Paul", she said, "it's the only thing that does work. Not the 'religious do-gooders' or the 'buy your way into heaven' stuff - none of it works except the thing you just read. God's love in Jesus.

Patty pointed out the window to the church across the park from the hospital they were in and said, *"**Paul, that's what Christmas is all about.**"*

She recognized his discomfort. He fidgeted and didn't look at her. She put a hand on his shoulder and laughed gently.

"Paul, I can tell I have made you uncomfortable with this topic of conversation. I tell ya' what, I'm feeling tired myself. Why don't we call it a day, and I'll see you tomorrow. Okay?"

"Sure", he muttered.

He got up and went back to his room. He sat down at the table and spent a good deal of time thinking about what he had just read.

"If only it were true", he thought. "If only it were true."

At bedtime, the nurse came in and took his vitals again. Then she gave him his medication, 'tucked him in' and he drifted off to sleep. But he didn't rest easily. There were too many questions, too many thoughts running through his mind, and too many things he wanted to talk to Patty about tomorrow.

And the uneasiness inside him only seemed to intensify.

He remembered how she had wanted him to go to church on Christmas eve, but he didn't think he was up to it.

He remembered that she had told him, "I'm going home soon" one afternoon while they were playing cards.

He thought she was saying she was getting better and would be released.

But it was obvious to him she wasn't.

He had felt a twinge inside of him, something he had never felt before. Not in this intensity.

"Are you well enough, Patty?", he had asked. He had been very concerned.

She smiled and said, "Not now, Paul, but I'm gonna be a whole lot better soon!"

Paul couldn't understand the look on her face, or the smile that radiated from her whole body, even though he saw a tear form and run down her cheek.

Across the park, the church bells had begun to play, *"Oh come, all ye faithful…"*

Patty seemed to weaken even more.

"I'm sorry, Paul", she said wearily. "I'm really tired. I want to sleep. I hope you understand."

"Of course I do, Patty", he had said and walked back to his own room.

He felt a great sense of uneasiness within him, but he passed it off as his own weariness. He relaxed and was soon asleep without having to take any medication.

During the night he woke up. His room was dark, but the curtains had not been drawn, and he could see colored lights on the window.

The door to his room was almost completely closed but a bit of light showed between the bottom of the door and the door jam.

He thought he heard the sound of frantic movement outside his room in the hall.

As he turned over, he saw someone sitting in the chair by table. He was wearing a white uniform like a nurse, but there was something different about him.

Sleepily, he asked, "Who are you?"

The man got out of the chair and came over.

Paul decided he was a male orderly. In the little bit of light Paul could see his beard.

"I'm here with you", the orderly said in a deep resonant voice. "Don't worry."

The orderly pulled the covers up over Paul's shoulders and went back to sit down.

In the morning, when Paul woke up, he was all alone. The nurse came in later than usual. As Paul looked at her. He could see that she had been crying. Her eyes were an angry red. She had something in her hands.

"Hi", Paul said to her. He had to force some cheeriness into his voice. He felt better this morning, but a sense of dread rose in him as the nurse told him she had bad news for him. She sat on the edge of his bed.

"Paul", she said hesitantly between sobs, "Patty died last night."

He felt as if he had been hit hard in the stomach. The nurse pressed something into his hands.

"There was a note among her things," the nurse continued, "and Patty wanted you to have this."

He looked at it. It was a notebook. He could tell by its appearance that it was well used. He opened it up.

There was a sticky note on the first page that read, ***"Paul, I pass on to you…the gift…the same one given to me. May you find the same joy and peace that I have known. I have made a list of some of the passages that have helped me deal with all the pain. I hope it helps you. Patty."***

He looked up into the eyes of the nurse.

"She knew she was dying. Didn't she tell you?", she asked.

"No", Paul said softly. "There was never a word. She did tell me she was going home soon, but there was nothing about dying. I thought she was referring to her health, that she was going to be released soon."

The nurse patted his hand and smiled sadly. "Then, she did tell you, in her own unique way."

Then the nurse stood up and was gone.

Paul reached over to the present Patty had given him and unwrapped it.

It was a Bible.

From the looks of it, it was about to fall apart. He opened it and found several passages that had been underlined. He read many of them.

About noon the nurse came back in with his lunch. He wasn't hungry and felt like talking.

"Who was the orderly that was in my room last night?", he asked her.

The nurse looked puzzled.

"There was no one with you, Paul. We were all in Patty's room trying to help her."

Now it was his turn to look puzzled and be confused.

"But...someone...an orderly was here in my room. He sat in that chair and came over to me and told me not to worry, because he was here with me. Then he covered me and sat down, and I went back to sleep.", said Paul.

"An orderly?", the nurse asked. "A male orderly?"

She was clearly skeptical.

"Yes!", Paul said emphatically. "Who was it?"

"Paul", she said, "We didn't have any male orderlies on duty last night. You must have been dreaming."

"No!", he insisted.

He was getting worried that she didn't believe him.

"I remember his beard – and his hands – I remember he had some really ugly red scars on his hands.", explained Paul.

She shook her head and said, "It may have been a side effect of your medication, Paul! Believe me, there were no male orderlies on duty last night. They were all given the evening off, because it was Christmas Eve."

Then she got up and left his room.

Paul thought long and hard about it.

He was positive he hadn't been dreaming.

"His hands...", he thought, "I know I saw...red scars."

And then it dawned on him.

He got up and went to the window of his room. Across the park people were leaving church and the bells began to play a melody from Handel's *Messiah,* ***"For unto us a child is born, Unto us, a Son is given..."***

The churchgoers looked blurry through his watery eyes, but he had never been able to see more clearly.

He finally began to understand the gift he had been given!

He turned and walked out of his room and into the hall. There was a smile on his face, and he felt as if nothing would ever be able to remove it again.

Paul walked into room #14.

There was someone new in the room, just getting unpacked.

"Hi!", he said. "My name is Paul. What's yours?"

About the Author

C.W. Pearson aka "Pastor Chuck" appears weekly on *Jam' n Java*, a popular internet broadcast, hosted by **#1 Hypeddit Recording Artist, Hammond® Organ aficionado**, keyboard player and music director for **Frankie Valli and the Four Seasons, Robby Robinson**.

C.W. Pearson serves as *Jam' n Java's* official on-air chaplain. Every Monday night, he touches countless lives, nationally and globally, via his **Christian** devotionals, preaching the *Word of the Lord*, seasoned with his own heavenly insight, original prayers and down-to-earth words of wisdom.

C.W. Pearson garnered worldwide attention with *Jam' n Java For the Soul: Book One* reaching #1 on six charts at Amazon. The book was featured in over **100,000+** media outlets and remains available globally at countless retailers.

A multitalented pastor, blessed with an abundance of gifts, he is currently working on *Jam' n Java For the Soul: Book Two*, as well as fictional works for youth and adults.

He holds a **Bachelor of Divinity** from **Concordia Theological Seminary** and a **Music Education** degree from **Western State University**.

As a stained-glass artisan, his crowning glory is a life size 6 x 9 stained-glass cross which adorns the outer entrance to **Trinity Lutheran Church** in **Simi Valley, California.** His religious and secular artwork is available on a smaller scale at **GodsGlassStudio** on **Etsy**.

If You Love Music and Faith You'll Love Jam' n Java

Hosted By Robby Robinson

#1 Hypeddit Recording Artist, Frankie Valli and the Four Seasons'
Music Director and Keyboard Player

Streaming Worldwide

Every Monday

7 p.m. Pacific, 9 p.m. Central, 10 p.m. Eastern

You Tube

www.youtube.com/JamnJava

facebook

www.facebook.com/jamnjava

www.ingramcontent.com/pod-product-compliance
Lightning Source LLC
Chambersburg PA
CBHW061502170626
46811CB00004B/1588

* 9 7 9 8 9 9 9 9 8 5 3 1 6 *